SNOW TROUBLE

G WALKER

SNOW TROUBLE

AND OTHER NEIGHBORHOOD STORIES
Compiled by the Editors
of
Highlights for Children

Compilation copyright © 1994 by Highlights for Children Inc.
Contents copyright by Highlights for Children, Inc.
Published by Highlights for Children, Inc.
P.O. Box 18201
Columbus, Ohio 43218-0201
Printed in the United States of America

ISBN 0-87534-632-4

Highlights is a registered trademark of Highlights for Children, Inc.

CONTENTS

CONTENTS

SNOW TROUBLE

By H. M. Myer

Tim's mother called from the kitchen, "Time to get up, Tim. It's eight o'clock."

Why was she calling him so early? It was Saturday, and he didn't have to go to school. Then he remembered. It was snowing hard when he went to bed last night. He and Brad were going to get up early and go out to earn some money shoveling snow off sidewalks and driveways. Tim needed seven more dollars before he could buy the hockey skates he wanted.

Quickly, he jumped out of bed and ran to the window. The snow had stopped falling, and the sun shone brightly—a perfect day to shovel walks. Tim put on his clothes as fast as he could and ran into the kitchen to have breakfast.

His mother was standing at the stove. "Hi, Mom," Tim said, sliding into his chair at the kitchen table. "Brad and I are going to make a lot of money shoveling snow today. I can hardly wait to get my new skates."

"Good morning, Tim," said his mother. "I'm sure you'll find plenty of sidewalks to shovel, but first I'd like you to clean our walk. Then there's a favor I have to ask of you."

Tim's mother brought his breakfast over to him. The bacon and pancakes sure looked good.

"As you know, Tim, Mrs. Keller next door fell and hurt her arm," Mother went on. "She's all alone with no one to help her. I really think it would be nice if you clear her walk after you have shoveled ours."

"Oh, Mom," Tim groaned, pouring syrup over his pancakes. "You know I'd be glad to shovel Mrs. Keller's walk, but can't I do it later? Brad and I want to get started before the other kids get all the jobs."

"No," said Tim's mother. "It would be best if you did hers first. Mrs. Keller will worry if her walk isn't shoveled, and she'll pay someone to do it. You know she doesn't have much money."

Tim silently ate his pancakes. He knew his mother was right. But if the other kids got all the jobs, he wouldn't earn enough money for those skates until another snowstorm came. The day didn't seem so bright anymore.

Tim finished breakfast, put on his parka and boots, and went to get the snow shovel. The snow was pretty deep. It would take a lot of shoveling to get all the snow off the sidewalk in front of his house. He shoveled as fast as he could.

When he had finished, Tim started in on Mrs. Keller's sidewalk. He heard something and looked up. Mrs. Keller was tapping on her front window. She waved at him and he waved back. He even managed a little smile. He knew it meant a lot to her to have her walk shoveled out.

Tim was just getting a good start on Mrs. Keller's sidewalk when Brad came up the street carrying his snow shovel. "Come on, Tim," he called. "We've got to go now if we want to get those jobs, or the others will beat us to them."

"Hi, Brad," said Tim, leaning on his shovel. "I'm afraid I've got some bad news. I have to finish Mrs. Keller's walk before I start the other jobs. It won't take long. How about helping me out?"

9

"Sorry, Tim," said Brad, "I can't wait. I've got to find a job that will pay me some money. You can do jobs for no pay if you want, but I've got to get some cash."

Brad turned and went on up the street. Tim felt worse than ever. Now, on top of everything else, his best friend was mad at him.

Tim had almost finished the walk when Mrs. Keller came to the door and called to him. "Tim, could you please come in the house for a minute when you've finished?"

"Sure, Mrs. Keller," he answered. Tim thought he might just as well. He probably couldn't get another snow-shoveling job anyway.

Tim finished the walk and went up on the porch. He stamped the snow off his boots and went into Mrs. Keller's house. She called to him from the kitchen. "I made some hot chocolate for you. It will be ready in a minute."

Tim took off his hat and mittens. The day was spoiled. Well, he would be polite anyway and drink the hot chocolate.

Mrs. Keller came from the kitchen carrying a steaming mug. She handed it to Tim and smiled.

"Thanks, Mrs. Keller," he said. "This looks good."

"I'm the one who should be thanking you," said Mrs. Keller. "I was so happy to look out this morning and find you clearing my walk. I knew you wouldn't let me pay you, so I thought of something else I could do for you."

Tim thought she was talking about the hot chocolate. But Mrs. Keller went on, "I thought I could help you by calling some of the neighbors and telling them what you were doing for me. Then I asked them if you could shovel their sidewalks, too. I have five jobs lined up for you this morning—and they'll pay you. Here's the list of names. So finish your hot chocolate. You've got a busy day ahead!"

"Wow! That's great, Mrs. Keller. Thanks a lot!" said Tim happily. "You're the best neighbor anyone could have." He finished the hot chocolate as fast as he could and pulled on his hat and mittens.

"Thanks again, Mrs. Keller," Tim said as he went out.

"You don't need to thank me, Tim. I thank you," she called, waving to him.

Tim picked up his shovel and ran down the street. He was just starting the first walk on the list when Brad came walking slowly by.

"Hey there, Brad," called Tim. "Did you get some jobs?"

"No," said Brad sadly. "Someone beat me to them."

"That was Mrs. Keller," said Tim.

"Mrs. Keller?" Brad acted as if he didn't believe his ears.

"That's right," Tim answered, smiling. "While I was cleaning her walk, she called the neighbors and lined up all these jobs for me."

"Are you ever lucky!" said Brad.

Then Tim had a thought. "Brad," he said, "there's plenty of work for both of us. Why don't you help me? Then we'll be partners again."

Tim smiled at Brad and held out his hand. Brad thought a moment and then smiled back. They shook hands, and together they started shoveling the walk.

Tim decided that he might not make quite enough money to get those skates this week, but there would be other snowstorms and lots more walks to shovel. He and Brad were friends again. That was more important. Tim started to whistle, and soon Brad joined in.

It was a perfect day.

THE FLOWER GARDEN THAT GREW

By Myrtis Bucy

Golpen Street was the most ramshackle street in the whole town. The fences were broken, the houses needed painting, and the porches sagged. Even the street sign was crooked.

Zelda Stevens of Golpen Street was one of twenty children chosen to attend a summer camp in the country for a week. And this led to the most thrilling experience of Zelda's life. A whole week of sunshine, clean air, green grass, big trees, and flowers was hers!

When it was time to return home, the woman in charge of the camp asked, "What did you enjoy most about your week in the country?"

Zelda didn't have to think even a minute. She knew what she enjoyed most. "Oh, I love the flowers—rows and rows of red ones, pink ones, yellow ones." Zelda's eyes grew large and happy as she thought of the flowers.

Then her face dropped as she remembered her yard at home. There was nothing but dirt, caked and crusted in the August sun—no flowers, not even a blade of green grass.

"Do you suppose," she began thoughtfully, "that flowers would grow in my backyard?"

"Of course," answered the camp director. "All you need to do is plant the seeds, give them some water, and the sun will do the rest."

"I don't have any seeds." Zelda's face became sadder.

"We can solve that problem," answered the lady as she took Zelda by the hand for a last inspection tour of the gardens. "Most of these flowers will ripen into seeds this fall. I'll gather some and send them to you in time for next spring's planting." And she wrote down Zelda's address.

A hot, dusty September followed the pleasant week at camp. But Zelda's thoughts went back happily to the well-kept camp and the beautiful flowers.

Early in November the snow began to fall, and for a few months the clean whiteness made even Golpen Street a prettier place. March, however, brought the spring thaws. Mud seemed to be everywhere. Golpen Street was in a most dismal state.

One Saturday morning the mailcarrier brought a large packet to the Stevens house.

"It's for Miss Zelda Stevens," her mother read.

"I've never gotten a package in the mail before," said Zelda wonderingly.

"Open it, child," urged Mr. Stevens.

Zelda undid the string and opened the package. Five small envelopes fell out. On each was a carefully printed word.

With a little difficulty Zelda pronounced each word, "Mar-i-gold, pe-tu-ni-a, cos-mos, zinn-i-a, nas-tur—"

"Nasturtium," prompted her mother.

Zelda's face beamed as she remembered the lovely flowers at camp.

"The camp director didn't forget to send me the seeds. Can I plant them today? Please, Mother."

"I don't see why not." Her mother smiled.

Zelda worked all forenoon, digging up a patch in the backyard. It was more of a job than she had thought. The ground had been packed by many feet and baked by many summers of sun. Finally, however, the ground was ready for planting.

"Those seeds will never grow," predicted one neighbor. "I never once saw a flower grow on Golpen Street."

But Zelda was not discouraged. She planted, watered, and waited for the sun to do the rest, just as the camp lady had said. One bright morning she saw the reward for her efforts. Pale green shoots were mushrooming up through the soil.

"How long will it be until I have flowers?" asked Zelda.

"I don't know," answered her mother. "I never planted a flower in my life."

Each morning before she left for school and each afternoon when she returned, Zelda inspected her garden. Then one afternoon, to her dismay, she found footprints everywhere in the moist dirt. Many of the plants were trampled. Wildly she dashed into the house.

"Mother, look at my garden!"

"I know," sympathized her mother. "All these years it hasn't mattered if the neighborhood kids ran through the yard. They just didn't think. They were running and playing. They probably never saw your flowers. Maybe the plants will straighten up."

"But what's to prevent them from running through the yard whenever they want to?" sobbed Zelda. "Oh, it's just no use."

Turning to her husband, Mrs. Stevens asked, "Couldn't you straighten that broken old fence a bit? It means so much to Zelda to have those flowers grow."

Mr. Stevens got his tools and began work on the fence. It was surprising how easy it was to repair. Then while he had the tools out, he fixed the broken hinge on the door, repaired the steps, and mended the screens.

The neighbors watched him for a while. Then they looked at their own dilapidated houses. One by one, they too got busy with hammer and nails.

By June, the first of Zelda's flowers started to blossom. By July the Stevens yard was a riot of color. It made the unpainted house look sadly out of place.

One evening when Mr. Stevens came home from work, he called, "I have a surprise for you."

"Show us, Daddy!" begged Zelda.

Mr. Stevens unwrapped a gallon of paint and a large paintbrush. "I'm going to start painting the house tomorrow morning."

The "prettying up" of the Stevens house and yard was contagious. Up and down Golpen Street, fences were mended and houses painted. One ambitious neighbor, caught in the cleanup fever, even ventured out with a stepladder to straighten the street sign.

"Look!" he called excitedly to his friends. "When I tried to straighten the *p* in Golpen, I discovered it was a *d* turned backwards and upside down. We don't live on Golpen Street. It's Golden Street!"

By now the name was really appropriate. All the windows shone, the grass grew, and people smiled. But the brightest spot on the whole cleaned-up street was Zelda's garden, where it all began.

You'll See

By Rosalyn Hart Finch

Sammy Sands hurried into the house. "It's time, Mother. Some of them are here already."

"They're right on schedule, aren't they?" Mrs. Sands looked up from her knitting. "Do you have everything ready for them?"

"Yes, but I'm going to gather it all together now."

"Good idea," his mother agreed.

Just then the doorbell rang. Sammy ran to open the door. "Hi, Mitch," he said to the boy standing on the porch. "What do you want?"

"Hi," Mitch replied. "Can you come out to play?"

"Not now. I have to get everything ready today."

"Get what ready?" Mitch asked, puzzled.

"You'll see," Sammy declared. "Would you like to help me?"

"Yes, I guess so," Mitch answered.

Sammy took a large brown paper bag from the broom closet. "This will hold everything," he said mysteriously. "Let's go to the basement first."

In the basement, Sammy first picked-up his red sand bucket, which was sitting on top of the clothes dryer. The bucket was filled with something gray and fluffy. "I've been saving this," Sammy said as he emptied the bucket into his paper bag.

"It looks like dirty cotton," Mitch declared.

"It's not cotton. It's lint from the dryer." Sammy smiled. "It's just perfect because it's so nice and soft and cuddly."

"I know what," Mitch cried. "Somebody's going to make pillows."

"Not pillows," Sammy said. "You'll see."

Next Sammy led the way to his mother's sewing machine. He opened a little drawer and pulled out a ball of string and a pair of scissors. He began cutting pieces of string about as long as his foot.

Mitch clapped his hands. "Now I know! Somebody's going to tie the strings around little balls of the dryer lint and make fringe like there is around the edge of my mother's tablecloth."

"No. You'll see, it's not fringe," Sammy insisted.

Next, Mitch watched Sammy tear an old pillowcase into little strips.

"Maybe somebody's going to make a rug," Mitch suggested thoughtfully. "My grandmother hooks rugs out of old rags and stuff."

"Wrong again!" Sammy chuckled. "It's certainly not a rug."

Mrs. Sands came into the garage. "Here are the pieces of red knitting yarn I promised that you could have, Sammy."

"Thanks, Mom. These will brighten up things a little."

Thoughtfully, Mitch looked into Sammy's bag. "It has to be some kind of stuffed animal. The red yarn is for the eyes, mouth, and tail."

Sammy shook his head. "You'll see," he said. "I have only one more thing to collect, and it's outside."

Mitch followed Sammy into the backyard. He was surprised to see Sammy take some twigs from the woodpile and drop them into his bag. Slowly Mitch shook his head back and forth. "I give up! I can't guess."

"I'll give you a hint," Sammy said. "All the things I've been collecting are building materials. They are for the new neighbors who have just arrived. Now can you guess?"

Mitch stared at Sammy. "New neighbors? What new neighbors?"

"You'll see," Sammy exclaimed, running to the back of his garden patch. "Help me spread these things out here on the ground."

When all the lint, strings, pillowcase strips, red knitting yarn, and small twigs had been carefully arranged, Sammy nudged Mitch and pointed up to a branch of the apple tree. "There are some of our new neighbors now."

"You mean those robins?" Mitch asked.

"Yes, they have just come from the South to spend the summer with us. They must start building their nests right away so they can begin raising their families. Mother said they will probably build right here in our neighborhood if I provide them with materials for a nest." Sammy grinned and pointed to a robin that had just flown down near a piece of red yarn.

Darcie
Dines Out

By Angela B. Haight

When Darcie's baby brother was born, Mom had to stay in the hospital for three days. Darcie thought that she and Dad would probably eat out on those days. She was looking forward to it.

"Great," she said, "pizza and hamburgers every night!"

"Well, not tonight," her father said. "The Spencers have invited us over for dinner."

Darcie put on a clean shirt, washed her face and hands, and combed her hair.

"Remember," Dad said as they walked across the street, "use your best manners."

"I know," Darcie said. "Say please and thank you."

"Right. And eat everything on your plate," Dad reminded her.

Inside the Spencer house Darcie sat at the table and sniffed quietly. It didn't smell like meat loaf. It didn't smell like lamb chops. It didn't smell like steak. What if it was something she hated?

"I'm so happy to hear about your baby brother," Mrs. Spencer said as she put a plate down in front of Darcie.

Darcie looked at the plate. Peas. That was OK. Buttered noodles. That was good. Some kind of gravy with chunks of meat and mushrooms in it. Darcie took her fork and carefully pushed the gravy away from the noodles and peas. Then she looked at her father, but Dad was already eating and didn't notice her. Darcie remembered what Dad had said about good manners. She took a tiny bite of meat. It tasted good! Soon Darcie had cleaned her plate.

"I'm so glad you like my beef stroganoff," Mrs. Spencer said.

"I've never had it before, but it was very good," Darcie answered.

The next night Darcie's father said, "The Fords have invited us over for dinner tonight." Darcie sighed. No hamburgers or pizza again. She washed up and walked next door with Dad.

As soon as Mr. Ford opened the door, Darcie could smell chicken. She loved chicken. Mr. Ford served her two drumsticks—"in honor of being a big sister," he said, winking at Darcie.

Darcie looked at her plate. Green beans. That was OK. Some funny-looking rice. It was brown and had red and green flecks in it with black blobs that looked like raisins. Darcie wondered why anyone would ever think of mixing raisins with rice.

Darcie ate both drumsticks very quickly. Then she polished off the green beans. She looked at the rice. Then she looked at her father. Dad was explaining something about his work to the Fords and didn't notice her. Darcie thought about good manners. She slid a few grains of rice onto her fork. It wasn't too bad. Next she stabbed a raisin and some more rice. It was really pretty good. Darcie ate everything on her plate.

The third night Darcie's mouth was watering for a juicy hamburger. Just as they were getting ready to go to The Burger Place, Mrs. Zappettini called and insisted that they come over to share "potluck."

"What's 'potluck'?" Darcie asked.

"It means taking your chances on what's being served," Dad explained. "Knowing Mrs. Zappettini,

I think we have nothing to worry about."

"But I just wanted to eat a hamburger tonight," Darcie complained.

First Mrs. Zappettini brought out a large tray of something she called "antipasto." Darcie was relieved to discover that it was really carrot sticks, celery, green onions, black and green olives, and pieces of salami. They all got to choose just what they wanted, so Darcie took several carrot sticks and some black olives.

At the dinner table Mr. Zappettini expertly twisted slippery strands of spaghetti into artistic coils on each plate and nestled big meatballs on the side. Then Mrs. Zappettini passed around hot, crusty bread. Darcie loved spaghetti. She thought the meatballs were almost as good as a hamburger, and the bread was better than a bun.

But then, oh dear! Mrs. Zappettini was bringing everyone another plate with a strange dark green thing in the middle. It was the size of a man's fist, with tightly closed leaves all around. Darcie touched it gently with her finger. It was tough and leathery, and the pointed ends scratched. Darcie thought about good manners. This was a special exception, she felt sure.

"It's an artichoke, Darcie," Mr. Zappettini said, pulling off a leaf. "Ummmm, good." He stuffed it into his mouth like a giraffe chewing leaves from a tree.

Very softly Darcie said, "I don't believe I care for artichokes."

"Try it," Mrs. Zappettini urged. "See. Pick off a leaf, dip it in the sauce, and then chew off the end. That's the tender part. Leave the rest of the leaf on the plate. Try it, Darcie. It's fun."

Reluctantly, Darcie picked off a leaf. She took a cautious bite. It wasn't bad. She tried a second leaf. Maybe it was pretty good. Soon she had a large mound of artichoke leaves at the side of her plate and a small cone of pale green leaves left in the center.

"Here's the best part," Mr. Zappettini said. "Let me show you how to get to the heart." Carefully, he pulled off the rest of the leaves all at once and handed them to Darcie just like an empty ice cream cone. Then he scooped out the center of the flat piece that was left on the plate, the heart. He cut it into several pieces.

"Now you can fix mine," Mr. Zappettini offered, so Darcie did. She was beginning to like artichokes.

"You're a good sport, Darcie," Mrs. Zappettini said as they thanked her at the door. Darcie smiled.

Walking home, Dad said, "I think we should have a special Welcome Home Dinner for Mom and the baby tomorrow night, don't you? I could go down to The Burger Place and get those hamburgers you've been craving."

"Oh, no, Dad," Darcie interrupted, "let's *really* surprise Mom. How about fixing beef stroganoff, brown rice with raisins, and artichokes for a change?"

Dad laughed. "She'll be surprised, all right."

"We'll just tell Mom that it's 'potluck,'" Darcie explained, "and see if she remembers her best manners as I did."

Basket of Friendship

By Pamela Schmidt Hodge

Mindy set the shopping bag on the sidewalk and stooped to pet the kitten.

"I bet you are Mrs. Matthews's kitty," Mindy said to the gray ball of fur playing at her foot. "You are far from home. Are you hungry?"

Mindy reached into the bag for the milk. She poured a small pool on the sidewalk and watched as the kitten lapped at the milk.

She petted the kitten good-bye and hurried home. As Mindy turned onto her street, she saw a big red moving van parked in front of a house. She had noticed the big FOR SALE sign in the front yard for weeks. Then one day a SOLD sign had appeared.

She watched the movers unloading some bicycles from the truck, and then she skipped home.

"Mindy, what took you so long?" Mother asked when Mindy got home.

"There is a new family moving in down the street. I watched the movers," Mindy told her.

"Please hurry and clean your room. Dinner is almost ready," Mother said.

Mindy hung her clothes and put away her toys. She put her shoes on the floor of the closet. Something brown in the corner caught her eye. She reached behind her clothes and pulled an old basket from the corner. She had used it as a bed for one of her dolls until she got a new bed for her birthday. The basket had been hidden in the closet for so long she had forgotten all about it.

Mindy was not quite sure what she would use the basket for now. But she was sure she would think of something! She put it back in the closet and hurried down to dinner.

By the time she finished her breakfast the next morning, she knew what to do with the basket.

Mindy placed her new coloring book and a box of crayons in the basket. Then she went next door to see Mr. Williams.

"What a nice idea," Mr. Williams said. "Here is a bunch of flowers I just picked from my garden."

Mindy thanked Mr. Williams and continued on to the rest of her neighbors. Mrs. Spalding added a freshly baked loaf of bread. Mr. Jones put in a good book he had just finished reading. Mrs. Ryan added a houseplant in a pretty blue-and-white pot.

"Here is a jar of applesauce," Mr. Brown said. "I made it myself from apples I picked from my tree."

Mindy carried the basket back to her house. She took a piece of stationery and a pen and she wrote: *Welcome to the neighborhood.* Mindy placed the note on top of the basket, loaded it onto her wagon, and rolled it down the street. She wanted the basket to be a surprise. She rang the doorbell and ducked behind the bushes.

"What is this!" the new neighbor exclaimed.

Mindy giggled. Her laughter floated out from the bushes.

"Someone is hiding in my shrubs. I wonder who it is."

"It is only me, Mindy. Hi."

"Come in, Mindy, and meet my children. I have a little girl just your age. And let us see what is in this basket."

Mindy took the lady's hand.

New neighbors are nice to have.

A THIEF
IN THE
NEIGHBORHOOD

By Kathleen West

He had lived in the neighborhood only four days, and already John was in big trouble. He was huddled against a tree, facing four angry boys his own age. They were all shouting at once and pointing at the camera he held in his hand.

"See, I told you so," yelled a boy named Mark. "He's the one who stole my camera. There it is."

"He thought because he's new in the neighborhood no one would suspect him," shouted another.

John was really scared. He hadn't stolen any

camera; but the one he was holding, the one his brother had given him for his birthday, looked just like the one that was missing.

"Let me have it! let me have it!" Mark yelled, grabbing for the camera. The other boys yelled, too, and pushed toward John, who held the camera even tighter.

He tried to tell them it was his, but they couldn't hear him. He felt someone's fingers pulling the camera out of his hands. Suddenly, there was a loud crash, and the shouting stopped.

The boys stepped back slowly. John looked down to see his camera smashed, the parts sprawled on the pavement. He felt sick inside.

"I tried to tell you the camera was mine," he said. "My brother gave it to me."

"You're a liar," Mark said, standing in front of John to keep him from picking up the pieces. "First you steal my camera, and then you try to lie your way out of it. You'll be sorry you ever moved into this neighborhood!"

With a swing of his foot, Mark kicked the camera down the sidewalk, watching more of its parts fly loose.

"You'll pay for this, kid. I promise you that." And he stalked away from John, followed by the other boys.

John began gathering up the pieces of the camera, but he knew it was beyond repair. As if it wasn't bad enough to have a broken camera, he now had all the other boys in the neighborhood angry with him. They would have been his friends, but instead they thought he was a thief—and a liar. How would he ever prove to them that he wasn't?

John didn't get much sleep that night, thinking about it. But finally he got an idea.

He didn't really want to take any money out of his bank. He'd been saving it to buy a new lantern to use on the family's camping trips. But he knew it was the only way to fix things.

The next morning he took out forty dollars, went down the street to the camera shop, and bought a new camera just like the one that had been stolen.

When he got home, John cut through the alley to Mark's backyard. By a huge oak tree was a roughly made clubhouse the boys used as their meeting place.

John looked around to be sure no one was there to see him, then he quietly went inside the clubhouse.

"If I leave this camera here, they'll find it and think it's Mark's. Then they'll stop blaming me."

He shoved the camera halfway behind an old orange crate.

"Here's hoping they find it soon," he said to himself.

The next day John was mowing the grass when the four boys rounded the corner and came straight toward him. His heart skipped a beat as he remembered Mark's threat. But they didn't look angry. They looked embarrassed.

John turned off the mower. Mark was the first one to speak. "Uh, John, we found my camera this morning. It was in our clubhouse by an old orange crate. I don't know how come we missed seeing it before." He shifted awkwardly from one foot to the other.

"What he's trying to say," said one of the other boys, "is that we're sorry we said you stole it."

"We didn't have any proof. We just picked on you because you were new."

John smiled. "That's OK," he said. "I'm glad you found it."

The boys smiled back, and soon they were all talking at once, trying to convince John they wanted to be his friends.

"Mark Jackson!" They heard someone yell and saw Mark's mother coming across the street. "Just look what I found in the back of your closet under your baseball glove." She handed something black to Mark.

"Why, it's my camera," Mark said, astonished. "How'd it get in my closet? We just found it in the clubhouse."

The other boys crowded around to look.

"I don't get it," Mark said. "How can there be two cameras? Unless . . ." He looked at John. "Did you put a camera in the clubhouse?"

John nodded his head. He was embarrassed. He hadn't wanted anyone to know.

"Where did you get that camera, John?" Mark asked. "We broke yours yesterday."

"Perhaps John bought another one," Mark's mother suggested. "Was it with your own money, John?" she asked.

This is awful, John thought to himself as he nodded his head yes.

The boys looked at him in amazement. "You mean you bought another camera for me," Mark said, "even though you hadn't stolen it, and after we had smashed yours?"

"Let's just forget about it," John pleaded. "You've got your own camera now, and I can keep this one I bought. Everything's cool. OK?"

"Not quite," one of the other boys said. "What about the money you spent?"

"Yeah, that's right," the others agreed. They looked at each other, then whispered something to Mark.

"Be right back," Mark said as he ran toward the clubhouse. When he returned, he gave some ten-dollar bills to John. "Hope that's enough," he said. "That's all we've got in the treasury."

John looked at the money and then at the boys.

"Sure, that's enough. But you don't have to . . ."

"I know we don't have to," Mark said, "but we want to."

They smiled at each other.

Mark's mother spoke up. "How about taking a picture to put on the clubhouse wall of all of you welcoming your new neighbor?"

"Good idea," said Mark. The boys stood together, and she took the picture.

Peter, Peaches, and the Porch Swing

By Linda Schultz

Peter wanted a letter of his own. He ran to get the mail each day as soon as it arrived. He waved to Mrs. Casey on her porch next door as he carried the mail to his mother. Every day his mother got mail, but there was never a letter for him.

One day Mother said, "Peter, please take this letter to Mrs. Casey. It came to us by mistake."

Peter ran to Mrs. Casey's yard and raced her cat, Peaches, to the porch. "A letter for you, Mrs. Casey."

"For me? Land sakes, no one ever writes to me.

Who could it be?" As Mrs. Casey read the letter, she slowly sat back on the porch swing. Peaches jumped to her lap and purred. "Oh dear, Peaches," she said softly. "They can't come to visit this year. Oh, Peaches, my sweet little friend." She scratched Peaches's ears as her voice faded away.

"Letters shouldn't make people sad," said Peter.

"Oh, Peter, I forgot about you. I'm sorry, dear. Here, have a cookie. And take some to your mother, too." She took some cookies from a small blue plate and wrapped them in a napkin. Peter took them home.

As Peter sat on his swing munching a cookie, he saw Mrs. Casey swinging very slowly. Peaches lay curled up on a rug at her feet.

Suddenly Peter had an idea. He got a piece of paper and wrote:

Dear Mrs. Casey,

   I like being your cat. I like it when you scratch my ears. I love you very, very, very, very much.

Your friend,
Peaches

And he mailed it.

When the mail came the next day, Peter heard Mrs. Casey laugh. She slapped her knee and laughed again. She called Peaches and scratched his ears. Then she waved to Peter. There was a piece of paper in her hand. "Hello, Peter," she called. "What a wonderful morning I am having."

Peter waved back. He smiled. His morning seemed brighter, too.

That afternoon Peter wrote another letter:

Dear Mrs. Casey,

I like being your porch swing. I like it when you rock fast. I love you very, very, very, very much.

Your friend,
The Porch Swing

And he mailed it.

When the mail came the next day, Peter heard Mrs. Casey laugh again. She slapped her knee and rocked so fast that Peaches scrambled out of the way. Then she opened a drawer in her table and took out a notepad.

The next day when Peter ran to get the mail, there was one envelope—with his name on it. Peter tore it open and read:

Dear Peter,

I got a wonderful letter from Peaches and another wonderful letter from my porch swing. I would love to get a letter from you. It would make me very, very, very, very happy.

Your friend,
Mrs. Casey

So Peter wrote Mrs. Casey a letter. But he didn't mail it. He delivered it himself the next day. And he and Mrs. Casey laughed, ate cookies, scratched Peaches's ears, and rocked very fast on the porch swing. And together they waited for the mail.

BLACKOUT BANQUET

By Beth Thompson

Clattering her spoon against the mixing bowl, Mrs. Wilkins scraped the last scoop of spicy-sweet pumpkin pie filling into the waiting piecrusts and popped them into the oven with a sigh of relief.

Mr. Wilkins had been called out with his crew to repair lines blown down across town. It was a terrible day to be outside.

"Mom, do you think that Dad will be home in time for our Thanksgiving dinner?" asked Jessica worriedly as she mixed the cranberry-orange relish.

"I hope so." As Mrs. Wilkins mixed the corn-bread stuffing, they listened to the radio.

"High winds tonight and continued heavy rain," announced the weather forecaster, "with a chance of local flooding." The storm seemed worse than ever, and the wind howled past the window.

"Josh, will you go check the basement for flooding," said his mom, "and, Jessica, you'd better sweep up those crumbs."

Suddenly the lights went out, leaving the house dark and gloomy. The radio was silent. And, for a moment, so were the Wilkinses.

"Hey, who turned out the lights?" shouted Josh from down below.

"Use the flashlight hanging on the wall," his mom called as she lit some candles. "Jessica, turn on your portable radio." She looked out the window. "There are no lights on in the whole neighborhood. It looks like a blackout."

"No water in the basement yet, Mom," said Josh, "but I stacked things out of the way, just in case."

"Well, the pies are done, but the oven isn't working now," said Mrs. Wilkins with a sigh.

"How will we cook the turkey and stuffing?" moaned Josh. "No dinner!"

Just then the phone rang. It was their neighbor,

Mrs. Carter. "This is a disaster!" she wailed. "My turkey isn't cooked and neither are my mince pies. I can't finish making my dinner."

"I know," said Mrs. Wilkins. "We're in the same fix. Maybe the power will be back soon. Tom and a crew have been out working since very early this morning."

"Those poor workers, out in this awful weather," said Mrs. Carter sympathetically. "That's not much of a Thanksgiving."

As the family waited for the lights to come on, they warmed themselves in front of a crackling fire in the fireplace.

"The Pilgrims didn't have electricity," said Jessica, "and they had a Thanksgiving feast just the same."

"Hey, let's cook our turkey over the fire the way they did," said Josh.

"We'll have to fix up some kind of grill," said Mrs. Wilkins thoughtfully, "and I'll cut the turkey into pieces."

"Hooray!" shouted Josh. "We can surprise Dad with a turkey dinner after all!"

"I'll wrap the stuffing in foil and cook it over the fire, the way we learned in Girl Scouts," said Jessica eagerly. "We can roast the corn on the cob."

"Dinner is saved!" said Josh.

"But not for everyone," said Mrs. Wilkins. "The

Carters don't have a fireplace and neither do the Hobarts. They will have to eat cold food, and their houses are probably getting chilly, too."

"We can ask them to come over here," said Josh.

"They can bring the food they've fixed, and we'll have a banquet," added Jessica happily, "just like the Pilgrims." Then her smile faded. "But what about Dad?"

"I hope he'll be home in time," said her mother. "He and the other workers will need some hot food by now."

As Jessica and Mrs. Wilkins set more places at the table, Josh phoned to invite the neighbors. Soon the room was crowded with smiling friends. Everyone drank hot cider and watched the turkey roasting on the fireplace grill.

The wind continued to hurl rain against the window, the power remained off, and there was still no sign of Mr. Wilkins. "I guess we might as well sit down to eat now," said Mrs. Wilkins finally. "I'm glad we're able to share this day with our good friends."

Suddenly, there was a knock at the door. It was a man from the power company, dressed in a dripping yellow raincoat. "Pardon me, ma'am," he said. "My crew will be working on the lines in your neighborhood. One of our men would like to use your phone to let his family know he's OK."

"Certainly," said Mrs. Wilkins. "He's welcome to use it. You're doing a fine job." She stepped aside to let the other man in. This man's rain hat was pulled low over his face. He walked to the phone and then hesitated.

"Excuse me," he said, "but do you by any chance know the Wilkinses' phone number?"

Mrs. Wilkins gasped, but before she could speak, Josh and Jessica were hugging the man in the wet yellow coat. "Dad! You're home!"

The rest of the crew came in, wiping their feet and shedding their coats, as Mrs. Wilkins and the others passed around hot coffee, hot cider, and food.

"It's the best Thanksgiving ever," said Jessica. And Josh, his mouth full of turkey, nodded in agreement.

The Grouch of Greentree Street

By Mary Jane Hopkins

Mr. Greeley grumbled and shuffled along Greentree Street. "Humph-h-h! It's too cold. Humph-h-h-h! It's too windy. Humph-h-h! The sidewalk is too cracked and bumpy."

Mr. Greeley pulled his thin coat around his stooped shoulders. He tucked his pointed chin into his upturned collar.

The children scurried to hide in doorways when Mr. Greeley passed. "Watch it!" they would shout.

"Here comes the grouch."

Mr. Greeley *did* look like a grouch. His narrow lips curled downward in a scowl. Bushy eyebrows almost touched in a frown over his dark eyes.

One day, however, as Mr. Greeley shuffled and grumbled down the sidewalk, one little girl did not run away. Her name was Annie. She had just moved to Greentree Street.

Annie huddled on the apartment steps and peeked at Mr. Greeley from behind the handrail.

When Mr. Greeley saw her looking at him, he paused to stare back at her for a moment. Then he shuffled away again.

The next day when Mr. Greeley took his daily walk, Annie was there again. This time her face flickered into a tiny smile. Mr. Greeley paused a moment and grumbled, "Humph-h-h." But when he walked on, he seemed to walk a bit taller.

Annie waited for Mr. Greeley again the next day. This time she greeted him with a bright smile.

Mr. Greeley paused and nodded his head ever so slightly. "Good day," he mumbled.

"Hello," Annie said.

And so it went. Day after day Mr. Greeley passed the steps where Annie waited. Her eyes sparkled when she saw Mr. Greeley.

"Mr. Greeley! Good morning." Annie would wave

and flash a big good-morning smile.

Mr. Greeley's shoulders didn't stoop so much anymore. He wasn't mumbling to himself either. His lips didn't curl into such a deep scowl, and his bushy eyebrows didn't hide a frown. "Good morning, Annie."

"Isn't it a beautiful day, Mr. Greeley?"

"A bit cold but, yes, a lovely day," he said as he tipped his hat and smiled a crooked smile.

After that, the children eased out of their hiding places one by one. They couldn't believe it. They had never heard the Grouch of Greentree Street say "Good morning" to anyone. They had never seen him smile before either.

And they had never even noticed Annie.

The children edged closer to Annie and smiled.

"Hi. I'm Michael."

"I'm Elizabeth."

"We're James and Tom . . . and this is Martha."

Annie smiled. "And my name is Annie."

The boys and girls gathered around her. "How did you do it?" they asked. Their voices bubbled with excitement. "How did you make the grouch smile?"

"Come back tomorrow and do as I say," Annie said. "I'll show you."

So the next day Michael, Elizabeth, James, Tom and Martha sat on the steps beside Annie.

"He's coming," they whispered, still frightened.

When Mr. Greeley saw all the children on the steps, he stopped. His scowl deepened again, and his bushy eyebrows met in a dark frown.

But then he saw Annie's sunshiny smile. All the boys and girls were smiling, too. They shouted, "Good morning, Mr. Greeley!"

For a moment everyone held his breath.

Then suddenly Mr. Greeley's frown disappeared. His scowl vanished, and he smiled the merriest smile ever.

"Good morning," he said. "And a beautiful day it is, too."

And no one ever saw the Grouch of Greentree Street again. He had turned into a friend.

THE GIFT GARDEN

By Nelda Johnson Liebig

Beth Reed ran into the house and hung her jacket in the hall closet.

"You're late," Mother said.

"Mrs. Hall asked me to go to the store for her," Beth answered.

"I'm glad you helped her. She and Mr. Hall haven't been well all winter."

"Did you know they have been married almost *fifty years?*" Beth asked.

"Yes, I am trying to think of an anniversary gift for them."

"We could paint their house," Beth said. "It needs it."

"That would seem as though we think their house is too shabby for our neighborhood," replied Mother.

"Oh, it is a *good* old house!" cried Beth.

Mother laughed. "You should know. You have been in every corner of it. They are like grandparents to you."

"Their garden sure is a mess with tangled weeds."

"They can't have a garden this year," Mother said. "It's just too much work for them now."

Beth remembered the big golden pumpkins that the Halls had given her each Halloween. "That's it!" Beth said, smiling. "I can ask everyone in the neighborhood to help plant the garden for the Halls. It will be a gift garden."

"That's a good idea, Beth, but you don't just drop seeds in a weed patch and watch them grow."

"Can't we clean it?"

"It must be cultivated," Mother said.

"Cultivated?"

"The dirt must be turned over with a shovel or a plow."

Beth knew she had to find a way. She talked with every neighbor on the block. They liked her idea, but no one had time to cultivate the garden.

Saturday morning Beth and her friend Mike pulled weeds. But Mike didn't stay long, and soon Beth was working all alone.

At lunch she washed her sore hands and sank down at the table. She could hardly eat her soup.

"Why such a sad face?" Mother asked. "What have you been doing?"

"Pulling weeds in the Halls' garden, but you are right. It is too hard." She tried to swallow the lump in her throat.

"Uncle Jim plows gardens, but this is his busiest time," Mother said.

"Please ask him anyway," begged Beth.

"I think *you* should."

Beth found the number and dialed. "Hello, Uncle Jim. This is Beth. May we borrow your plow to help with a gift for Mr. and Mrs. Hall?" She told him her plan. "Thank you, Uncle Jim." She put down the phone. "He will be out of town on Saturday and says we can use his tractor."

The next day Daddy said, "Beth, I'm sorry, but Mr. Hall told me they don't need a big garden anymore."

Beth blinked away her tears. There wouldn't be a garden! She wished she had never thought of it.

Suddenly she knew what to do.

Wednesday evening the neighbors met at Mr. and Mrs. Hall's house. The Reed family brought a pretty cake with pink-and-white frosting. Others brought cookies and punch.

Beth and Mr. Hall looked at each other and smiled. It was time to tell their secret.

Mr. Hall said, "I wonder whether any of you would be interested in using our garden?"

"A neighborhood garden?" asked Mother.

"Yes. Everyone plants and everyone shares," he said.

"Oh, I always wanted to have fresh green beans," said Mr. Lake, "but my yard is much too small for a garden."

"Mine, too!" agreed Mrs. Hanson, who lived in a tiny apartment.

"It was Beth's idea," Mr. Hall explained.

Everyone smiled at Beth. Her face turned red, but her eyes danced with happiness.

"It will be fun," said Mrs. Hall. "This fall we will have a harvest supper in our yard. Corn, pumpkin pie, squash, tomatoes, cabbage, potatoes—all from OUR garden."

Beth laughed. "We wanted to give *you* a gift, but you are giving a gift to the neighborhood."

"Well, that's what neighbors are for," Mrs. Hall said with a smile.

UNDERGROUND RIVER

By Jean Waldschmidt

Philip was in the barn helping his father when old Mr. Withrow came storming in.

"So, here you are, John Stephens!" he said angrily to Philip's father. "That bull of yours broke my fence *again* this morning, and we just chased fifty head of your cattle off my grazing land."

Philip's father dropped the barbed wire he was rolling. "Listen, Mr. Withrow, the drought has burned up my grass, and we're hauling water to keep the cattle alive!" he said hotly. "You have grass and water because of the spring-fed brook that runs through your place. My half-starved cattle are going to try their best to get at it!"

"That's no concern of mine!" Mr. Withrow snapped. "I'm warning you, the next time I find any of your herd on my place, they'll be shot!" He turned and stomped back to his truck.

Philip's father watched him drive away in a cloud of dust. "I wish WE had a brook that never went dry," he said bitterly.

Mr. Withrow's brook came from underground streams that trickled together until finally they made a river. The river came to the surface in the form of a spring right in the middle of the Withrow range.

"Dad, maybe that river runs through our place," Philip said thoughtfully. "Why don't we drill a well and see if we can tap it?"

His father smiled. "It costs money to drill wells, Philip. If we were to hit a couple of dry holes, it would just about finish off the Stephens ranch."

Philip sat down to think. How did you go about finding an underground river, he wondered. He knew the early settlers, traveling by covered wagon, had a way of locating water. Everyone in the wagon had watched for a willow tree or a clump of green bushes. Maybe HE could do the same thing.

The next morning Philip saddled his pinto pony. He rode over the ranch for hours, but he didn't see any willow trees. And hungry cattle had long ago chewed the leaves off what bushes there were. At the end of the day, he was tired and discouraged.

The next morning he saddled his pony again and rode out toward a natural rock formation called The Knob. Philip's father had told him that probably an earthquake millions of years ago had caused the rock to erupt there. A narrow road ran along beside The Knob, separating the place from Withrow's.

The Knob! Philip thought excitedly. Why hadn't he thought of it before? Maybe that same earthquake had formed an underground passageway. And maybe underground streams had trickled into it and turned it into a riverbed! Philip spurred his pinto to a gallop.

But when the huge rocks came into view, he felt his heart sink. Always before, The Knob had been a riot of color because of the wild flowers that grew in its crevices. But now only parched brown stems remained. There wasn't any water here.

Then he forgot his disappointment as he heard men's voices. Riding closer, Philip saw that a cattle truck was parked crosswise on the road. Withrow's fence had been cut, and a ramp let down from the back of the truck into the pasture. Men on horseback were shouting as they herded the Withrow cattle toward the waiting truck.

Philip stiffened in his saddle. Those men weren't buyers! If they were, Mr. Withrow would have had the cattle penned up in the corral waiting for them. They would be loading from a chute, instead of cutting the fence.

Those men were stealing the Withrow cattle! It would serve old man Withrow right, Philip told himself. With his fat, sleek cattle gone, Mr. Withrow would be in the same shape as the other ranchers.

The sound of men's voices grew closer. "Hiyah! Hiyah!" they shouted. Philip could hear the slap of a whip against a cow's back. He heard a calf bawl. When he heard the whip crack again, he knew he couldn't sit there and see the Withrow's cattle stolen. He'd never feel right inside if he did.

"Quiet, boy," he said softly to his pony. He slid noiselessly off the pinto, and staying behind the rocks, he crept close to the road.

What could he do? By the time he rode for help, the cattle would be loaded, the truck gone. Philip knew he'd have to figure some way to keep the truck there.

Just then the driver and the man he'd been talking with strolled to the fence to watch the men rounding up the cattle. If the driver had left the keys in the truck . . .

Philip bent low and ran across to the truck. He jumped lightly on the running board. The keys were dangling from the dashboard! With one quick motion he jerked them out and sprinted back to his waiting pony.

"Hey, look over there! There's a kid!" the driver yelled in surprise.

But Philip had jumped on his pony, and the keys were safe in his pocket.

"Fast, boy!" He spurred his pony and took the barbed-wire fence in a leap.

"Get him!" one of the men yelled. But Philip was safely headed across open country.

It seemed hours before he reached the Withrow house and gasped out his story. Mr. Withrow and his men piled in a jeep and hurried to The Knob. The cattle truck was still there, but the rustlers were gone. Some of the Withrow hands went on in the jeep to overtake them, but Philip and Mr. Withrow stayed with the men who were starting to fix the fence.

The truck still straddled the road, the back end in Mr. Withrow's pasture, the front touching the Stephenses' property at the foot of The Knob. Philip stared at the front end of the truck. The heavy wheels were sunk down a couple of inches in the dirt. This land was soft—soft as if water flowed beneath it! He knelt down and began to dig around the truck wheels.

"It's the underground river!" he yelled. Mr. Withrow came running. "It goes beneath The Knob on our land and comes out in your pasture!" Philip held out the clump of moist dirt.

Mr. Withrow took the dirt and rolled it in his fingers. "I believe you're right," he said finally. "Probably never would have found it if that heavy truck hadn't parked right on it."

Then he clamped his hand on Philip's shoulder. "For a long time we've needed water in this corner of the range." Somehow he didn't sound cranky, as he usually did. "You tell your dad, Philip, that I'm going to drill a well right here where our land meets. It's going to have a double faucet, one on your side and one on mine. That way, we can both have water!"

"Wow! That's nice of you, Mr. Withrow. Thanks a million," Philip said. "I know my dad will be grateful to have a well out here." And Philip quickly mounted his pony and headed toward home to tell his father all that had happened.

WENDY'S TREE

By Karen Cummins Pida

There's a set of rules on my street that all the kids follow. Age matters, size matters, and climbing up Wendy's tree matters most.

I'm almost eight, and I'm small for my age, so I get treated like a little kid. They say, "You're too small," and "You haven't climbed up the Tree yet." I know things will change once I climb it. They'll listen to me. I'll get to make some of the rules.

"I'm going to climb the Tree," I bragged to my big brother one night while we were setting the table for dinner.

"Right," Larry said with a snicker. "Sure you are."

"I am!"

"In what century?" he said.

Mom called from the kitchen, "All right, you two. What's going on?"

"She thinks she's going to climb Wendy's tree," answered Larry.

"That big old maple with the rickety tree fort, Jessica?" she asked as she came into the dining room. Mom had the look on her face that she gets when she's worried.

"You have to swing, too, you know," Larry said. "No fair using a ladder either."

I glared at him. "I *know* the rules. I won't go all the way up to the tree fort part, Mom. I'll just go up to the swing part."

"You don't know the secret of how to climb it," Larry said mysteriously.

"What secret?"

He just smiled.

"It must be seven feet to the lowest branches!" Mom said, giving me a little hug.

"It's not dangerous, Mom," I said.

"You might have to wait until you're older, Jessie."

"Yeah," Larry said, laughing. "Like maybe until you're fourteen."

I looked away.

Maybe Mom was right. I was scared . . . a little. What if I only made it partway up, or fell? What if everybody laughed?

If I could just practice when no one could see me, I thought. I remembered my first few piano lessons. I wasn't very good. But after I practiced, my first recital went perfectly, without a mistake. It's too bad you can't practice climbing a tree.

Well, why couldn't I? I could get up real early and try.

The next morning, I saw the Tree from my yard. I ran to Wendy's house like an Olympic athlete training to win a gold medal in tree climbing.

When I got there, the Tree suddenly seemed taller and much too wide for a kid my size. I had never been so close to it before. Usually, I watched from across the street.

I looked for the best side to try. Walking around and around the old tree, I chose the side with thick roots covered in ivy.

My cheeks were hot. My skin prickled. The only sounds were my breathing and the squeaking of my wet sneakers. Even the birds were asleep.

I hugged the cold, hard trunk, wishing giant arms would magically lift me into the branches. The Tree felt strong, old, and scratchy, like the scales of a dragon.

I slipped on the damp roots. I scratched my arm on the pieces of bark. I couldn't even stay on the dumb roots. Stupid tree!

Tears came, and everything was blurry. I don't care about making rules anyway, I thought. I should just leave. No one knows that I came here. But I wanted to get up that tree.

I wiped my eyes and took a deep breath. I had to try again. I pulled at the peeling bark.

That's when I saw a little black ant. All alone, it scaled the trunk like a tiny mountain climber. It kept disappearing into the Tree, into caves of bark. Then I could see it again, higher, up on the trunk.

"If that ant can climb this big tree, then I can, too!" I said, right out loud. The ant kept climbing higher and higher up.

I stared at the trunk. The bark wasn't really peeling. It hadn't come off when I pulled. Pieces of bark stuck out from the trunk. *Hundreds* of them. They made handholds and footholds up the tree, like a giant staircase. Giant for an ant, maybe, but just the right size for me!

What a great secret! In just a minute or two, I scrambled right up that tree.

I stood on the natural platform where the trunk split. I felt good—as if I had won that gold medal. I could have stayed up there forever, or climbed even higher. Then I saw the rope swing waiting. The next step, right?

I wished all the kids were there to see me. But it didn't really matter. I had climbed the Tree. I knew the secret. That was enough for me.

I grabbed the rope, and with a Tarzan yell, I swung down and out, over the grass and into the sky.

Sarah's Mistake

By Sister Mary Murray, H.M.

Sarah ran into the house and right into her mother's arms. "The girls from Cherry Hill School told me it would be like this. I didn't believe them," she sobbed. "But they were right! People don't want us in this neighborhood. They don't!"

"Come, sit down, honey," her mother said softly. "Tell me what happened."

"Wait, Mom. See that girl on the porch across the street?" Sarah pointed. "I wanted to make friends with her the way you and Daddy said I should. So I waved and said hi. I even held up my jump rope.

But do you know what she did? She just turned off her cassette player and walked in the house."

"Did you say anything else to the little girl, Sarah?" asked Mother. She was worried, but she didn't want Sarah to know it.

"No, I didn't! And I'm not going to either. She can just keep on playing her silly old cassettes."

"Look, Sarah," said her mother gently. "Let's give her a little time. She may be shy."

"Old stuck-up, that's what she is!" Sarah's eyes kept filling with tears. "Momma, I want to go back to Cherry Hill School. These kids will never play with me."

"Hush, dear!" said her mother. She put her arms around Sarah. "This doesn't sound like our little girl. You love your new house. You have your own room. You have a place to study and a place to play. Everything will work out. You'll see."

But things did not work out for Sarah. Day after day passed, and the girl across the street took no notice of her at all.

One afternoon, the two girls met in an ice-cream shop at the mall. The girl's father was talking to her. "Let's see, Gabrielle. How about lime sherbet? Or orange? Or maybe raspberry."

"Oh, Daddy, I love raspberry," said the girl. Suddenly she bumped against Sarah, but the girl pretended she had never seen her. "Pardon me, please," was all she said.

Sarah didn't answer. "Stupid," she thought. "Who does she think she is—a movie actress or something—with her red dress and dark glasses? Gabrielle? Ugh!"

The first day of school finally arrived. Sarah was excited. She stood at the front door, waiting for her mother. Suddenly she cried out, "Mother! Come quick. Look! Gabrielle isn't even going to my school."

Sarah was correct. She and her mother watched while Gabrielle boarded a blue-and-gray bus in front of her house. On the side of the bus in large letters were these words: DR. GRAY'S SCHOOL FOR GIRLS.

Sarah's mother sighed. "We'll make the best of it," she said, almost to herself. "There will be other friends, honey."

Sarah said nothing. But suddenly she decided she didn't like Gabrielle at all. "I'll show her," she muttered, "Just wait till I get a chance."

The chance came sooner than she expected. The next afternoon Gabrielle was sitting in her yard listening to cassettes and playing with a tiny black puppy. Suddenly, the puppy jumped from her arms.

71

"Come back here, Peppy," she shouted. "Come back. Where are you going?" Gabrielle jumped to her feet and started after the puppy.

At the same time, Sarah rode down the sidewalk on her new bike. "Watch where you're going," shouted Sarah. "Look out!"

But it was too late. The bicycle had brushed Gabrielle, and she fell.

"What's the matter, klutz? Don't they teach you safety rules in that silly school of yours? Or can't you see?"

"No," said Gabrielle, starting to cry. "I can't see. I'm blind!"

"Blind!" gasped Sarah. "You're blind?" She put down her bike and helped Gabrielle to her feet. "I'm sorry I said what I did," said Sarah. "Here, let me help you. Then I'll get your puppy. My name is Sarah, and we just moved in across the street."

"Yes, I know," said Gabrielle. "My mother told me. I was hoping we could play together, but not everyone likes to play with blind people. I can't even go to your school."

"That Dr. Gray School is—" began Sarah.

"For the blind," said Gabrielle. "We learn to read with our fingers and listen to stories on cassettes. I have a story today called 'The Giggling Ghost of Haunted House Three.' Would you like to hear it?"

"I sure would," said Sarah. "But wait till I get your puppy and tell my mother where I am. Is she going to be surprised!"

The
BLUE BOX
for SABBATH

By Marilyn Leitner Reiss

Every Friday Jonathan helped Mother prepare for the Sabbath. While Mother finished making the house tidy and clean, Jonathan polished the heavy brass candlesticks. He helped set the table, putting out the silver wine cup and arranging the challah bread under its cover. Then, just before Mother lit the Sabbath candles, Jonathan would drop a quarter into the blue box on the shelf.

Jonathan had been quite small the first time he had put money into the box. "What is this for?" he had asked Mother.

"This is the charity box. Every week, to make the house ready for Sabbath, we put money in the blue box. The money helps people in our neighborhood who are poor and in need."

Each week, after he dropped in a coin, Jonathan shook the box. He liked the cheery jingling sound. He liked to think of all the people who would be helped.

This Sabbath the house was tidy, the table set, and all was ready. Mother put the thick white candles into the brass candlesticks and struck a match.

"Stop, Mother! You forgot the blue box. You didn't give me a coin to put in the box!"

"Come and sit with me a minute, Jonathan." Mother looked sad. "You know that things are difficult for us right now. Your father doesn't have much work these days. I haven't been able to give you money for ice cream lately. David can't take violin lessons anymore."

Jonathan nodded. "And no money for movies on Sundays," he said.

"Yes," Mother said. "We've cut down on everything we could, but still, each week, we have put money in the blue box. But now," she sighed, "until things get better, we will have to give up the coin for the blue box."

Mother covered her head with a shawl. She lit the candles, raised her hands before them, and sang the prayer in Hebrew. But somehow, though the candles flickered and danced, they did not glow with their usual Sabbath joy.

That night Jonathan had a dream. Mother had told him many years ago about the good and bad angels that visit every Jewish home on the Sabbath. If the house is ready and the family is pleasant and kind, the good angel will say, "So may it be all week and also on the next Sabbath," and the bad angel must agree by saying, "Amen." But if the house is a mess and the children are cross and quarreling, the bad angel will say, "So may it be all week and again on the next Sabbath," and the good angel is forced to agree by saying, "Amen." That night Jonathan dreamed that the bad angel had shaken their blue box. No coins jingled. Jonathan awoke.

"We *must* have money for the blue box." Jonathan decided. "I'll ask David tomorrow."

David often teased Jonathan, but when Jonathan explained about the money for the blue box, David could tell that this was serious. "I'm sorry, Jonathan, but I can't help you. I haven't had an allowance for months." He thought a moment. "How about doing odd jobs for the neighbors?"

"Thanks!" said Jon as he turned and raced to Mrs. Green's.

"Well," said Mrs. Green as she thought over Jonathan's idea, "if you'd like to earn some money, how would you like to do my shopping for me? It's hard for me to get out with the baby. I'd give you a fifty cents a week."

Jon nodded happily. "I'd like that."

Going out again into the frosty air, Jonathan thought, "Mrs. Green is paying me because she can't get out to shop herself. Who else is there? I know! Mr. Simon!"

"Oh," Mr. Simon sighed. "That would be wonderful! It is so hard for me to get to the store. But no," he shook his head, "you are doing this to earn money. And I haven't any to spare. I'm sorry. I could not give you even a nickel."

Jonathan was disappointed. But suddenly he remembered—charity was not only money for the poor, it was good deeds, too. Maybe doing things for Mr. Simon would count, even if he didn't have any money for the blue box. "I'll be glad to do your shopping for you anyway, Mr. Simon," he said in his most grown-up manner.

Thursday afternoon, Jonathan went to the grocery store with two lists, a long one from Mrs. Green and a short one from Mr. Simon. He looked at Mrs. Green's list. "Wait a minute!" he thought. "I can get coupons for some of these things at home!" Jonathan raced home. Moments later he was going down the aisles, putting packages and cans into his cart. When he got to the check-out counter, he said, "I have some coupons. I get fifty cents back." The cashier took his coupons and handed him two shiny coins.

Carefully balancing the two bags, Jonathan knocked at the door of the Greens' house. "Thank you, Jonathan," Mrs. Green said, "and here's your fifty cents."

"Wait, Mrs. Green. I used some coupons and got money back, so you don't have to pay me."

Mrs. Green slipped the quarters into Jonathan's pocket. "You earned this money," she said. "I'll see you next week."

Then Jonathan went to Mr. Simon's house. "You did a good deed, Jonathan. Tell your mama. She should be proud of such a boy," Mr. Simon said with a smile.

Friday afternoon Jonathan polished the brass candlesticks carefully. He set the silver wine cup and the braided challah on the table. Then he slid his coins into the slot on the top of the blue box. They jingled happily as they fell in. As Mother lit the match, Jonathan remembered the happy light in Mr. Simon's eyes as he thought of not having to go out into the cold to the store. The candles had the same cheerful light.

Jonathan knew the good angel had won this week. He turned to his family. "Good Sabbath!" he said. And it was.

The Soup That Made Itself

By Rose-Marie Provencher

Mrs. Flynn sang to herself as she bustled about her spick-and-span kitchen. *Bingety-bang, clickety-clack* rattled the pots and pans in time to the her happy song.

But as the clock struck two, Mrs. Flynn stopped singing. She tweaked the white window curtain into place and then took down from the shelf her favorite soup pot.

Thursday night was ALWAYS noodle soup night in the Flynn household, because noodle soup was

Mr. Flynn's favorite food. All year long, every Thursday night, that is what they had for supper.

Mrs. Flynn filled the shiny pot with water and set it on to boil. She set out salt and pepper, a nice plump chicken, and a package of noodles. She smiled. It would be a GOOD soup.

Suddenly Mrs. Flynn stood still. "Oh dear," she said with a frown. "I forgot to take Molly Muddle-by that recipe. Well, it will take only a moment."

Quickly she hung up her apron. Next she gave each of her four red geraniums a drink. Then she hurried off to Molly's house.

"My," she said, giving her hair a last-minute pat, "I'll have to hurry right back, or my soup will never be done in time for supper."

Back in the spick-and-span kitchen, the sun shone warmly through the window, making the geraniums look bright and happy. A breeze made the perky curtain dance. On the stove the water in the pot went *bubbly-bubbly-bubble,* bouncing the cover up and down with little puffs of steam.

A tiny mouse that lived in the house had just come out to nibble some crumbs when a knock at the door scared him back into hiding. It was Mrs. Nosey, a friend of Mrs. Flynn's. After knocking three times, she opened the door and called, "Yoo-hoo, Matilda."

Now Mrs. Nosey was nice—but nosy. And when she spied the pot on the stove, she just had to know what Mrs. Flynn was going to have for supper. So she peeked under the cover and found only water bubbling away. Then, spying the chicken, she said, "My, Mrs. Flynn means to have chicken for supper, but she has forgotten to put it in the pot. Well, I'll just do it for her," which she did. Then she went home.

The little mouse had just gathered up enough courage to pop his head out again when there came another knock at the door. This time it was Mr. Purdy. Getting no answer, he opened the door. On the stove sat the great soup pot going *bubbly-bubbly-bubble.*

"Oh dear," thought Mr. Purdy, "I really shouldn't, but I would so like to know if Mrs. Flynn can cook chicken better than I." So he tiptoed over to the stove, removed the cover, and spooned up a sip of the broth. "Oh, my goodness!" exclaimed Mr. Purdy, "she has forgotten the salt and pepper! It really tastes quite flat." So he salted and peppered the soup and replaced the cover. Then he went home.

Slowly the whole kitchen became filled with the delicious smell of stewing chicken. The breeze made the curtains whisper against the screen. The little mouse nibbled away. The pot cover bounced up and down. And the sun shining through the window made the geraniums glow even redder. Then came another knock at the door.

The mouse scampered for his hole, the door opened, and Mrs. Bright Eyes peeped around the corner. "Oh dear, I guess Mrs. Flynn isn't at home," she decided. "But I wonder what she can be cooking for supper." She lifted the pot cover.

"My goodness, it's chicken soup," exclaimed Mrs. Bright Eyes, "and she has forgotten to put in the noodles. I'm sure she won't mind if I help a bit." So she emptied the noodles into the soup. Then Mrs. Bright Eyes hurried home, for the sun was going down and it was getting late.

Mrs. Flynn, hurrying along the path toward home and supper, wore a worried frown on her face. "Oh dear, oh dear," she said. "I should never have stayed so long. What will Mr. Flynn say when there is none of his favorite soup for supper?" And she worried all the way home.

Then, turning the last twisty corner, she met the most wonderful nose-tickling smell. "Why," said Mrs. Flynn, stopping in her tracks, "I can't believe my nose! THAT smells like noodle soup—but it CAN'T be!" And she ran across the yard, up the steps, and into her spick-and-span kitchen.

There on the stove bubbled the big soup pot, full of chicken noodle soup! Mrs. Flynn tasted it. It was JUST right.

"Good gracious, how can this be!" she exclaimed. "Who . . . how . . . when . . . ?" Mrs. Flynn looked around, but there was no one to tell her who had made the soup. The four red geraniums knew, but they couldn't tell her. The little mouse knew, but he couldn't tell her either. "Did you make yourself?" she asked with wonder.

Just then the door opened. Mr. Flynn was home. "Ah," he said, with a big smile and a hungry sniff. "Noodle soup night!" He took off his coat, washed his face and hands, combed his hair, and sat down at the table.

Mrs. Flynn put a big bowl of soup at Mr. Flynn's place and a big bowl of soup at her place. Then she sat down, and they both began to eat.

Mr. Flynn smiled happily across the table at Mrs. Flynn. "I don't know HOW you make such delicious noodle soup every time," he said with a merry wink.

"Why," winked Mrs. Flynn right back, "it's very easy. In fact, you might almost say THIS soup made itself!"

Mr. Flynn tipped his head back and laughed right out loud at such a funny idea.

But Mrs. Flynn laughed even louder because how a soup pot full of JUST PLAIN WATER had turned into a soup pot full of just-right noodle soup was still a mystery to her.

Neighborhood Day

By Paul Tulien

The Wilson children were playing in their shady front yard after an early breakfast. They had just said good-bye to their mother, who was on her way to work.

It felt as though it was going to be another hot summer day.

A neighbor hurried by, carrying a paper bag.

"Hello, Mr. Darby," Jimmy Wilson called. "Where are you going?"

Mr. Darby paused a moment. "I'm going on a picnic. It's a holiday today."

"Holiday?" asked Jimmy's sister, Lisa. "What holiday is it today?"

"It's the ninth of August."

"What holiday is the ninth of August?"

"August 9 is the Ninth of August, just as July 4 is the Fourth of July."

"But the Fourth of July is Independence Day. What is the ninth of August?"

But Mr. Darby, who was a little deaf, had gone on and was already out of hearing range.

"I never heard that the ninth of August is a holiday," Lisa said. "Let's go in and ask Grandma."

Grandma was making cookies.

"What holiday is it today, Grandma?" Lisa asked.

"It isn't any holiday."

"But Mr. Darby said he was going on a picnic because today is a holiday."

"He must have been joking." A little later Grandma added, "I suppose it could be a local holiday. Maybe this town was founded on this day, so they're celebrating. We've lived here so short a time we wouldn't know about it. I wonder why none of the neighbors has said anything about it."

"Where will they have the celebration?" Lisa asked.

"In the park, I suppose."

"Are we going?" Jimmy asked.

"No, I guess not."

"Why can't we?"

"Yes, Grandma, why can't we?" Lisa asked.

"Well, I suppose we could. While the cookies are baking, we can make some sandwiches."

In a short time they were on their way. Mrs. Green looked out her front door. "Where are you going so bright and early in the morning?"

"Mr. Darby said he was going on a picnic because today's a holiday."

"What holiday is that?" asked Mrs. Green.

"I'm sure I don't know." Grandma answered, chuckling. "I thought it might be some local holiday, but maybe he was just joking."

"He must have been. Well, have a good time. I wouldn't mind going on a picnic myself."

"Why don't you? We'd like company," Lisa said.

"It would take too much time to get ready. The two youngest of my six aren't even up yet."

"Let me help." Grandma said. "If it's a joke, I wouldn't want us to be the only ones fooled."

"Thank you! My children would enjoy it. They're always saying there's nothing to do. Mr. Darby was joking, but we can have a good time anyway."

When the other children in the neighborhood heard about the picnic, they ran home to ask their parents if they could go, too. Before long the news had spread all through the little village.

By noon most of those who didn't work in the city were in the park. Even the owners of the stores and shops had closed their doors and come. But Mr. Darby, who had started it all, wasn't there, and nobody knew where he was.

Everybody had fun. The children played games while the grown-ups sat on benches and talked. And many were surprised at how many new friends they made that day.

At sundown Mr. Darby came home after spending the day fishing down by the river. Everybody wanted to know what he meant that morning when he said it was a holiday.

"I was just joking," he said, surprised at what he had started. "I finished a painting job yesterday, and it was so hot I wanted a day off before I began another job."

In the evening Lisa asked, "Why can't we do this every year? In July we have the Fourth. In September we have Labor Day. But in August we just don't have anything."

Others asked, too—not just children but many grown-ups as well—because they had all had such a good time that day. And so everyone decided to celebrate again next year. But since the "Ninth of August" doesn't seem to be much of a name, it will be called Neighborhood Day.

Bobby Sniffs Around the Block

By Lucy Fuchs

Bobby loved dogs. On Bobby's birthday Dad came home with a brown dog with floppy ears. The dog was excited when Bobby took her. She wagged her tail and licked Bobby's face. She sniffed Bobby all over. She sniffed at Mother and Dad, too.

"Thanks for the dog," Bobby said to his mother and dad. "I'm going to name her Ginger."

"You'll have to feed her every day and give her baths," said Mother.

"Oh, I will," said Bobby.

Bobby showed Ginger his room. He showed her all around the house. Ginger sniffed at everything.

"Mother," Bobby asked, "why does Ginger sniff at everything?"

"That is how she learns to know things," Mother said. "She knows things by their smell."

Bobby sniffed the air. "I think I'll try that, too," he said.

When Bobby woke up the next morning, he thought of Ginger. Then he closed his eyes again. He sniffed hard. "Bacon and eggs for breakfast," he called to Mother.

"Come and see," Mother said. Bobby was right. They were having bacon, eggs, and toast with butter and jelly.

Mother brought him a large glass of milk. He sniffed at it. It smelled cold and good.

He sniffed at Mother. She smelled like a mother— clean and sweet and a little bit like buttered toast.

Bobby's dad was reading the paper. Bobby sniffed at the newspaper. "Did it rain this morning?" he asked.

"Yes, it did," Dad said. "Very early this morning. How could you tell?"

"The paper smells like rain," Bobby said. He sniffed at Dad. Dad smelled like shaving cream.

"You'd better feed Ginger," Dad said when they had finished breakfast.

Bobby sniffed at the dog food. It smelled like meat, but not meat for people. He took it to Ginger. He sniffed at Ginger, and Ginger sniffed at him.

Bobby and Ginger took a walk around the block. They both sniffed at everything. When they came to the field where he and Paul and Rich played ball, Bobby closed his eyes and sniffed hard. It smelled like dirt and balls and fun.

They walked on to Mrs. Brown's flower garden. Again Bobby closed his eyes and sniffed. Ginger sniffed, too. Mrs. Brown's garden smelled like roses and lilacs.

Mrs. Brown was working in the garden. "Your garden smells good," he said.

"Thank you," she called, and she went back to her work.

Next to Mrs. Brown's flower garden was Mr. Jones's vegetable garden. Bobby and Ginger sniffed hard. Bobby could smell onions and tomatoes and strawberries. Mr. Jones was watching him. "What are you doing?" he asked.

"I'm smelling your garden. It smells like food," Bobby said. Ginger barked and wagged her tail.

Bobby and Ginger walked on past more houses. They sniffed at the trees as they went. Some trees smelled exactly like Christmas trees. Others smelled like nuts and acorns.

Bobby stopped in front of a little store. He closed his eyes and sniffed. He smelled spices and fruit and many other good things. He smelled peppermint candy and jelly beans. Ginger sniffed and wagged her tail.

Bobby went on and on. At last he stopped in front of a little yellow house. It was the house of the Smith family. He sniffed. He smelled something funny. It was something that was wrong. He smelled smoke.

He ran to the door and rang the doorbell. Ginger barked. Mrs. Smith came to the door in an apron. "I smell smoke," he told her. "Maybe your house is on fire."

Mrs. Smith laughed. "Come and see," she said.

Bobby and Ginger went with her to the back of the house. There she was burning some leaves. "See, that's where the smoke you smelled came from," Mrs. Smith told Bobby.

"But I have something for you," she said as she went into the kitchen. Bobby closed his eyes when she brought it to him. He sniffed. He smelled something cold and sweet and delicious. And he smelled chocolate.

"Chocolate ice cream!" he cried.

"No," said Mrs. Smith, "take a look."

In a bowl was white ice cream covered with chocolate syrup.

"Thank you, Mrs. Smith," Bobby said.

Ginger sniffed and barked. She wagged her tail. Mrs. Smith looked at Ginger. Then she got a dog biscuit for her. Ginger barked to say thank you.

"Thank you both, Bobby and Ginger, for smelling my fire," Mrs. Smith said, smiling. "But now I think that you two had better sniff your way home."